3
Tales
Cynan Jones

TALES

CYNAN JONES

ILLUSTRATED BY
ROHAN DANIEL EASON

Gomer

First published in 2018 by Gomer Press,
Llandysul, Ceredigion SA44 4JL

ISBN 978 1 78562 233 5
A CIP record for this title is available from
the British Library.

The Piano Player's Hands was selected for
Richard and Judy's Winning Stories and first published
by Chrysalis Books in 2003

This book is published with the financial support of the
Welsh Books Council.

Printed and bound in Wales at
Gomer Press, Llandysul, Ceredigion
www.gomer.co.uk

For whoever you may be.

THE PIANO
PLAYER'S HANDS

The Piano Player was asleep when his hands woke up and began to argue.

That day he had given a terrific concert, his best ever, everybody said. People had clapped and clapped while he waved his right hand to the crowd with pride, his left hand casually in his pocket out of sight, or mopping the sweat from his brow with a silk hanky.

In the night, while the Piano Player snored like someone playing a tuba in the bath, his hands started to talk.

"Thank you for supporting me today," said the Right Hand, tired after his dazzling performance.

And the Left Hand was angry.

"Oh!" he said, sarcastically. "My pleasure."

"What's the matter?" asked the Right Hand.

"You're always the star," said the Left. "You always get the beautiful tunes. I've heard people whistling them after our concerts, walking away from the hall. Nobody notices the work I have to do, down there, below you ... plod, plod..."

It was not the first time they had argued.

"At least you don't always *have* to entertain people," said the Right Hand. "It's tiring. And sometimes I get bored of playing the same things, the same few tunes over and over during a piece, so people *can* remember them, and whistle them to themselves. You change everything depending on what you play – while I just decorate the same thing."

"But you get the applause."

"Only because I am more obvious."

"I want applause. I want people to notice me. And it's not just in concerts either. It's in everything. You're his favourite."

"What do you mean?" asked the Right Hand.

"He waves you to the crowd."

"And you wipe the sweat from his brow."

"You hold his glasses of champagne when he stands in parties."

"And you scratch an itch, or brush away a fly."

"You shake the hands of the politicians he meets, and the princes and important people."

"And you hold his child when he walks in the park."

Sometimes the Right Hand envied the Left. It was true he was more dazzling – had more attention in crowds, or was called upon for grand gestures; but he sometimes wished for the simple tasks he never seemed to earn. Things which to him seemed more important. That happened to keep a person comfortable.

"You keep his wedding ring safe, and wear his watch," said the Right Hand.

"I have to pick his nose!" argued the Left.

"And I wag a finger at his child when he misbehaves in the park."

The Left Hand found it difficult to understand why the Right Hand felt so sorry for himself.

The Right Hand loved the fact that the Left was more free to change because nobody watched him so much, and they did not really expect things. For half a song he might plod, plod, repeating the same line underneath a high tune. But then - when people had almost forgotten him, when he had become more part of the piano than part of the music - he would change gently, and make everything different. And people would be moved, surprised, lulled as they were, expecting nothing, concentrating only on the obvious.

"Maybe we should swap," said the Left Hand. And they agreed.

And so it was that one day, on the morning of a big concert, the Piano Player woke up and found himself in terrible trouble. He tried to clean his teeth, but his hands just would not work. They simply refused. Trying to tie his shoelaces was a disaster. And so was trying to eat his boiled egg for breakfast. He spent the whole day tripping over and hungry!

By the time the Piano Player arrived at the concert hall, he was a nervous wreck. He even had to ask a viola player to tie his bow tie for him, which took quite some time! "It will be okay for the concert," he kept saying to himself, "it will be okay..."

But it wasn't okay. The concert was a disaster.

The Right Hand smiled roundly as he played beautiful chords and arpeggios and counter melodies, little snatches of the tune, louder or quieter, loving the way he changed the music. The Left Hand thundered around the bass notes, banging out the famous tunes too low for people to whistle, or trilling and turning round special notes, proud to show the audience that he too could dance. But it sounded like a lorry reversing, or a rumbly tummy. The Piano Player was very distraught.

When the concert finished, nobody clapped. Some of them put one hand or the other to their mouth to whistle rudely, or threw their programmes to the stage in disgust. Nobody put their hands together to show appreciation – to show their happiness as they usually did. And the Piano Player's hands felt very, very selfish.

They knew then they were one as important as the other. That they were not the same, and couldn't do the other's work. They realised that they were made different so they could support one another, to create something complete. And they didn't fight anymore.

From that day on, each hand concentrated only on what made them special, and didn't try to be something they were not. And the next concert, because of that, was the greatest ever heard.

THE SCARECROW
AND
THE DOLL

Not too far away from here, there once was a magnificent field of flowers, taller than the tallest person that you know, and the colour of a carnival parade.

Passers-by would stop and stare, their eyes lit up, watching the wind shift the sea of shades, believing themselves on a butterfly's wing.

Noses filled with scent, and ears with the sea-sort-of-sound of the leaves; and with their eyes shut, people pretended they danced - *rustle, rustle* – by a princess in a long silk dress.

Painters came from miles around, and lords with picnics and picture takers. Poets poured out words. Whether people chattered like chaffinches or went very quiet, the flowers affected them all.

One morning some children from a tiny town came to play in the flowers. Careful to stay at the edge of the field so they could always find their way out, they hid and sought and hide-and-seeked, buried themselves under petals.

All day they laughed and played, gathering together the stalks in wide arms to make thick trunks like trees; tracking paths that gypsies might have traipsed down in old fairy tales. And when they heard the bell, beat five times from the church in the town, they left the field of flowers.

It wasn't until later, when it was time for bed, that one little girl knew she'd lost her doll. She had left it in the flower field, dressed in a lace white gown.

The doll stayed where she was for some time in case the girl came back. But when she didn't, the doll decided to try to find her way home. There was the soft petal hush of the flowers around, the canopy of colours. The flowers were so thick above the doll she hardly noticed night fall.

By the time she realised it was quite dark, the doll was completely lost.

The moon came out and dropped through the flowers, lighting the floor with silver, like ten pences in a wishing well. And the doll walked on, secretly wishing as well.

When, amongst the hushness, she heard a sharp sound like a stick breaking, she suddenly grew very afraid. It was a sound like an old witch clicking her fingers, or a skeleton's clattering bones.

She couldn't help walking more quickly, thinking of the things the sound might be, forgetting how pretty the flowers were as the fear picked her up like a wave. The thoughts of what the noise could be turned into a chasing, scary dog. And then she started to run.

Pushing the flowers apart, aside. Knocking the petals loose. Tearing the leaves, until – with the shock of falling into a hole – she stumbled into a clearing.

And there, staring down at the doll, a towering scarecrow stood.

She froze, and did not move...

The scarecrow thought the doll would scream, but she stood quite still and silent.

All around the wind sushed and the flowers swayed uneasily, losing their colour as the moon went in. With no idea of what to do, the doll sat down and cried.

"I've frightened you," the scarecrow said.

"No," said the doll, being brave. Her head was hidden in her lace white dress.

"Then why do you cry?" the scarecrow asked.

"I'm lost," the doll replied.

The scarecrow did not know what to do. At least, he did not think that he did. But he did the right thing and spoke.

"It's a long time since I cried," he said. "Before the field was full of flowers."

The little doll looked up.

"The farmer came and ploughed the earth and broke the soil and then, while the field still hurt, scattered seeds across it. He made me out of old clothes and bits of straw and stuck me in the ground. I've been here ever since.

"People looked at me and laughed. Threw stones. 'Look at his ugly face,' they'd shout, 'and his beggar's clothes'.

"I scared away the birds that nowadays dance above the field catching flower seeds. 'Wait,' I used to shout. 'Wait.' But they would fly away."

The doll sat silently and listened to the story. Her own tears dried. She felt as if she was the first person the scarecrow had ever really told this to.

"I stood through rain and storms and sun that burnt my eyes. I could not move, because I am only built to stand the way I am. And when the first shoots appeared, I scared away the nibbling rats and scurrying mice and slimy slugs and snails, making myself so ugly even they would not come near.

"I cried, when no one was looking, because I thought perhaps I was only guarding cabbages, or sprouts, and the pain would not be fair.

"But as the shoots grew, I began to know they would be something beautiful. Soon they grew too strong for rats and mice to harm, so I let them play among the stalks; and the birds simply rested on them, stopped picking off the buds, waiting to see what the field would become.

"I cried again on the first day a flower appeared. My tears fell into the soil and helped the flowers grow, one by one, until they filled the sky around, protected me from the wind and rain, and hid me.

"Today, when people come, I hear their voices as they look across the field. I do not mind they have forgotten I am here. But I can tell they are the same people who threw stones at me, once upon a time. All they see now are the beautiful flowers.

"I am not needed now. But here I am."

"In case something nasty comes again," said the doll. "You are part of the flowers."

"Are you still frightened?" the scarecrow asked.

"No," said the doll.

❧

THE UNBENDY GIANT

Now, this was a long time ago. In fact, it was *once upon a time*, which is when all these things seemed to happen.

There was a giant. He wasn't a nasty giant, but he was really incredibly big.

"I can see for miles," he would say, deafening the poor people below him. "I can see so far, I can even see what comes next!"

Now, having a giant about wasn't such a bad thing. The people got on with him well, and accommodated him as best they could. And in return, he would help when they needed something done.

If they needed to plough their fields, the giant would pluck out an eyelash and scratch it up and down the ground a bit.

If they needed to build more houses, they would climb up a big hill and shout: "We need more houses! Would you get us some gravel?"

Then the giant would reach over to the beach, or a rocky mountain slope, and pick up a great handful of stones and put them down where the people asked.

(They had to say 'gravel'. To the giant, 'stones' would be giant-size stones).

He was very useful for watering crops too, but that's not something to put in a nice story like this.

Now the giant knew he was very much bigger than everyone else. Everyone else was you-and-me size. And because they were you-and-me size, it took them a long time to get up and down hills to talk to the giant.

He could have bent down to listen. But he knew if he did, he wouldn't have a moment to himself. So he pretended he could only stand upright. At least he got some peace that way.

'Anyway, they wouldn't be doing what they do if they could see things from up here,' thought the giant. Little things seemed silly to him.

As he got more and more tired of helping them out, he made people walk up bigger and bigger hills.

"I can't hear you," he'd say. "As you're aware, I can't bend down. You'll have to climb something higher." And so he had more time to himself. And time to yourself – as you probably know – is when you have silly ideas.

'What the little people need is a bit more direction. It's obvious what they want. It would be much better if I did their thinking for them. And it would mean I'd know where they were all the time, so I wouldn't have to worry about treading on them.' (It really had got tedious, having to worry about that).

"Right then!" he said. And he declared himself 'Protector'.

"I will look after you," he proclaimed. Protector of the Little People. And there wasn't much they could do about that.

For a while the you-and-me size people still wasted time running up and down trying to talk to the giant. But he would just say:

"Don't worry, leave it to me. I can see what you want from up here. I have a better idea of it than you."

And when they still kept coming to talk to him, he just went splat, splat, splat with his hand, and flattened out the hills. So they couldn't talk to him anyway. There was no way they could get close.

'This is much better,' the giant thought.

From way up where he was, the giant couldn't hear a thing the you-and-me size people said. No matter, though, to him. He thought he knew what he was doing.

Now, because he was Protector, that made him quite important. And as you know, important people have to wear nice clothes.

'Mmm,' the giant thought, 'I'd better look the part.'

So he ordered all the tailors and dressmakers and leatherworkers and weavers to make him a new outfit.

'I better keep my strength up too,' he thought, 'now I have all this responsibility.'

And he ordered the farmers to grow more food, and the cooks to cook massive plates of all the things he liked to eat.

In a way it was good, as everybody was suddenly very busy, working for the giant.

But the giant ate more in a bite than the you-and-me size people ate in a week, and soon the food was running low.

"Go and get that crop from over there," the giant would say. And the people would have to set off for miles to fetch the extra food. (He could have done it himself, but... Well. He was *important* now).

"You have to build your houses bigger too," said the giant, "so I can see them better. I wouldn't want to tread on them."

So it made sense to build them all together in a block, as many as they could. That way the giant could clearly see where people lived.

"That's better," he said. Except suddenly there were lots of people in quite a tiny space. And because all the ground in that place was covered with houses, no-one had room to grow their food. So they had to be supported too.

The other problem in these new living places was there wasn't anything *real* to do, now people weren't busy growing food and mending carts and looking after animals. So the giant made up jobs to keep them busy.

One job was Making Holes in the Sky; another was Moving Shiny Little

Pebbles from One Place to Another for No Particular Purpose. But the people were led to believe, of course, that these jobs were very important, and they went about it busily.

'Mmm,' thought the giant again, looking out across the horizon. 'I can see lots of other land from up here. Given how busy everything is getting, we could do with some more. We need more fuel for all this cooking too...'

So off went the people, at his behest, to get more land. (It was fine, the people in the other place had no giant to protect them, so there wasn't much trouble).

'This is really working very well,' thought the very big giant to himself.

Soon, the dressmakers had spent so long making giant clothes they forgot how to make things normal size. And the cooks were used to cooking such big plates they couldn't scale it down.

It wasn't long before all the people were walking round in too-big clothes and eating far too much.

But the giant didn't mind. There were so many people running round for him he didn't really notice. Besides, it had been a very long time now since he'd seen a you-and-me size person anywhere near up close.

Perhaps the strangest thing was that a lot of people, most in fact, started to think the giant was right. After all, they didn't have to make decisions anymore.

They just did as they were told. As long as they were not getting squashed, everything seemed okay.

In what was really no time, no-one was left to remember what things were like before the giant had taken charge. Just following him along was normal. They believed now he was *necessary*.

One day a little boy, quite out of the blue, asked: "Isn't this all wrong? Mum and Dad look after me because I'm littler than them, and I look after my pet mouse because he's littler than me. But we run round after the giant. We spend all our energy making things his size. It should be the other way about. He could do the work of lots of us if he wanted to be helpful."

"You better watch yourself," somebody said. "He could crush you with his foot."

"He's trying to look out for us by telling us what to do, to make sure he doesn't step on us, which is awfully kind of him," said another.

"And as long as we obey, we're safe."

"It doesn't sound quite right," said the little boy.

"Well, I don't want to get squashed," said the somebody else.

"No, nor do I," said the boy. And things kept growing on a giant scale.

Now, giants live very much longer than people you-and-me size, and very soon – in giant time – the giant had started to rely on other people doing everything for him.

But things started to go wrong.

First, it took so long to make his clothes that by the time one thing was finished, he'd worn out something else. So he never had a matching set.

To try and make things happen faster, he made more and more people work, even people who had no idea how to do a thing. So things didn't get made properly and started to fall apart.

Second, the food was running out because people had grown fat. More and more people had to be sent around the land gathering new crops and finding space to farm. And in doing so, they upset more and more people that were living quite happily until they arrived.

The further they went, the more living spaces sprang up, and before long – in giant time, again – there were so many you-and-me size people running to and fro that the giant couldn't move. He couldn't take a step for fear of crushing them.

'What have I done?' he thought. 'I think I might have got it wrong. Things have got out of hand.'

"Okay, stop!" the giant said.

But it's not easy stopping what you've started. Many of the people now could only do one thing. So if he asked them to stop doing it, they just sat about quite miserably. This wasn't ideal at all.

"Has anyone got ideas?" the giant asked. But due to his plan, not many people had ideas left anymore.

"Just go and farm and leave the towns. We'll take things apart and start again. You can sort yourselves out now."

This is what the giant said. But no-one could remember how to do the little things by then. 'I better get down to their level and hear what they have to say,' he thought.

But when he tried to bend his back he found he couldn't do it. He had been pretending that he couldn't bend for such a long time that he was all seized up.

"Come and tell me what to do," he said, quite nervously. "If any of you have ideas, I need to hear them now."

But even if there had been mountains left, the people were too fat to climb them. Mostly, the people looked on stumped, staring up at him.

"I can't get down to you, and you can't get up to me," groaned the giant, desperately wobbling back and forth as he tried to bend.

"I can't stay here like this. I'll have to try and move, try and loosen up."

So up came a very big foot and down it came, crash, and crushed a factory. Then the other foot, crunch, destroying several farms.

He kicked over schools and hospitals, and put his foot through mines. "What's going on?" the people cried, scattering away. "Somebody talk to him." And the giant stumbled round, crushing more and more under his feet.

"He's not much of a Protector now," the people cried, most of them quivering inside. "He's destroying everything we built. We have to talk to him."

And the giant groaned and knew he was in trouble. The situation was impossible. The only choice the people had was to bring the giant down.

"We'll have to trip him up," they said. "Then we can shout into his ear."

Now, can you imagine what a mess there was when the giant finally fell over?

Acknowledgements

Many thanks to Cathryn Gwynn, who saw the value of these tales, and to Ashley Owen for her careful eye. Also to Rohan Daniel Eason for his illustrations, Meirion, Gary and all at Gomer.

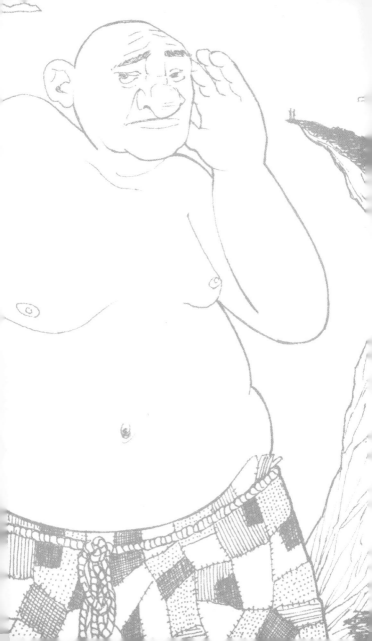